Catholic School Girls

by Casey Kurtti

A SAMUEL FRENCH ACTING EDITION

SAMUEL FRENCH

FOUNDED 1830

New York Hollywood London Toronto

SAMUELFRENCH.COM

Dedicated to
WALTER HADLER

DOUGLAS FAIRBANKS THEATRE

LUCILLE LORTEL and MORTIMER LEVITT
in association with
BURRY FREDRIK and HAILA STODDARD

present

CATH⬯LIC
SCHOOL GIRLS

A New Play by

CASEY KURTTI

with

LYNNE BORN   **MAGGIE LOW**

SHELLEY ROGERS   **CHRISTINE VON DOHLN**

Setting by
PAUL LEONARD

Lighting by
PAUL EVERETT

Costumes by
SIGRID INSULL

Associate Producer
BEN SPRECHER

Directed by

BURRY FREDRIK

Originally produced at the White Barn Theatre, Westport, Connecticut

4

The Off Broadway Production of CATHOLIC SCHOOL GIRLS opened at the Douglas Fairbanks Theatre on April 1st, 1982.
The cast was as follows:

ELIZABETH MCHUGH/SR. MARY THOMASINA
.... LYNNE BORN
WANDA SLUSKA/SR. MARY AGNES . MAGGIE LOW
MARIA THERESA RUSSO/SR. MARY GERMAINE
.... SHELLEY ROGERS
COLLEEN DOCKERY/SR. MARY LUCILLE
.... CHRISTINE VON DOHLN

CHARACTERS

Colleen Dockery/Sister Mary Lucille
Maria Theresa Russo/Sister Mary Germaine
Wanda Sluska/Sister Mary Agnes
Elizabeth McHugh/Sister Mary Thomasina

AUTHOR'S NOTES

CATHOLIC SCHOOL GIRLS is obviously a memory play. It is my intention that the audience drift in and out of that reality. That is why there are no costume changes when the students "become" their teachers. When casting, the director should not be concerned with the youth of the actors, the concern should be with a strong ensemble. (Technically the Catholic school girls would be in their early thirties.) In addition, I would like to point out that the text is very well suited to non-traditional casting and I vigorously encourage you to do so. In the Off-Broadway production we used very realistic props, costumes, sets, etc.; however, in Australia everything was left to the imagination. Either way, the play works.

TIME: 1962–1970

PLACE: St. George's School, Suburb in New York State.

Catholic School Girls

ACT I

SCENE: Music begins playing as lights gradually come up on a Catholic school first grade classroom in 1962. There are six student desks in a row. An oak teacher's desk and chair, a wastebasket and an American flag by its side. A blackboard, two bulletin boards, a crucifix and a big clock decorate the backstage wall.

AT RISE: After a few moments, ELIZABETH, COL-LEEN, WANDA, and MARIA THERESA Enter. They are dressed in white uniform blouses, blue ties, white cotton slips, knee socks and brown oxford shoes. They are carrying their uniform jumpers. They each stand by a student desk and begin to dress as the music continues. They look around the classroom and at each other as they dress. Then ELIZABETH raises her skirt to pull her blouse down neatly. all follow suit, straightening their blouses. When they are finished ELIZABETH shouts.

ELIZABETH. I'm ready!

(The lights come up quickly. The music stops. It is the first day of First Grade, 1962.)

COLLEEN. (*polishing apple, while watching MARIA THERESA crawl under a desk*) Where's the teacher? I wanna get started.

WANDA. I saw the teacher in the bathroom. She said to pick a seat.

MARIA THERESA. The teacher's in the bathroom? (*COLLEEN begins to eat the apple.*)

WANDA. She's throwing up.

COLLEEN. Boys are supposed to sit over there. You retarded or something? What's that?

ELIZABETH. My mother pinned it on me. It's a Holy Medal for the first day. I live on Remsen Road in an apartment—

COLLEEN. (*to MARIA THERESA:*) I live near you.

COLLEEN. You got that white car with the back door off. It's a circus car right? Right?

ELIZABETH. I have four brothers and two sisters. We ARE going to get a house—someday.

MARIA THERESA. No!

COLLEEN. You live down by Carvel's. I seen your family there, your father's fat.

WANDA. I know where Carvel's is . . .

ELIZABETH. (*crosses to statue*) Hi, Jesus. Come here, Mr. Gunderson, say hi.

WANDA. Who's Gunderson?

ELIZABETH. My friend, she stays with me. Mr. Gunderson is a girl. She's got a red dress on, with lots of bows. She doesn't like this uniform.

COLLEEN. I don't see her.

ELIZABETH. She's invisible to people.

MARIA THERESA. (*Waves furiously in wrong direction and crawls under desk again.*) My name is Maria Theresa Russo.

ELIZABETH. She has long hair.

MARIA THERESA. I see it.

WANDA. Is she your sister?

ELIZABETH. No she's my friend. I don't talk to my family.

COLLEEN. (*Crosses to front.*) I have my own room. My brothers are slobs. They jump on the couch when my mother is not home. We are the only Catholics on the block, the rest of the families are Jews.

WANDA. I know some Jews.

COLLEEN. Shut up. My second best friend, Kitty, is a Jew. She has a little doll house with lights that turn on and off and —

WANDA. There were lots of Jews where we used to live.

COLLEEN. (*getting furious*) They go to church on Saturday and they all go to public school.

MARIA THERESA. When is the teacher going to stop throwing up? I don't like it here.

COLLEEN. That's a sin, you have to go on Sunday, right? Right?

ELIZABETH. I don't know.

COLLEEN. Well I do, because I'm going to be a nun. Got a little doll that's a nun. Sister is going to let me try on her bride's veil . . .

MARIA THERESA. Do they have any hair underneath that bride's veil?

WANDA. Oh yes.

COLLEEN. Who says?

WANDA. Mamow — My Mother. She taught me a special hymn for the first day to sing to sister, wanna hear?

COLLEEN. No.

ELIZABETH. Yes.

WANDA. The Ave Maria by Wanda Sluska . . . Zdrowa's Maryo, Laskis Pelna, Panz Toba . . . (*air raid siren sounds*)

COLLEEN. Yuch, stupid name.

MARIA THERESA. Lunch time, already?

ELIZABETH. That sound means the communists are sending a bomb over here. We all have to go home.

WANDA. But we just came here.

COLLEEN. This is Cheez Whiz. What you got? I'll trade you.

MARIA THERESA. I have a meatball hero. I think this is my sister's lunch.

ELIZABETH. There is a bomb shelter in my apartment building. I got to call my grandmother so she can get on the bus and come over to my house before it goes off. She lives in the Bronx. My grandfather isn't coming, he's already dead. You guys can come over and hide, but no boys allowed.

WANDA. We are supposed to hide here.

COLLEEN. Who says?

MARIA THERESA. We have bunk beds. Maria Diana sleeps on top of me. Maria Rose sleeps on top of Maria Ann. Anthony sleeps on top of Salvador Jr. Cosmo sleeps on top of Joseph.

ELIZABETH. Red fiery stuff comes out of that bomb and if it falls on you it could burn your skin right off. (*MARIA THERESA pulls out sweater.*) That won't save you. You need a raincoat.

WANDA. I'm getting the teacher. (*Exits*)

ELIZABETH. This Chinese guy got hit by the bomb the last time while he was riding his bicycle. He got squished right into the ground. You can go over there and see him right now. He is still lying there all flattened out with his bicycle.

COLLEEN. (*stops eating*) Is the guy dead?

ELIZABETH. Yes.

COLLEEN. Hey, wait for me.

ELIZABETH. One second. (*She grabs Jesus.*)

MARIA THERESA. I'll get the mother.

COLLEEN. Don't touch the snakes, they could come alive. (*SISTER MARY AGNES Enters.*)

SISTER MARY AGNES. Boys and girls. My name is Sister Mary Agnes. (*Writes it with the holy water.*)

MARIA THERESA. Sister, are you finished throwing up?

SISTER MARY AGNES. What was that, dear?

COLLEEN. I gotta ask you something about that bride's veil.

SISTER MARY AGNES. Take your seats, First Graders, and good morning. My name is Sister Mary Agnes.

MARIA THERESA. Sister, there is a bomb coming over here. We're going to this girl's house. You wanna come?

SISTER MARY AGNES. This is just a test. We hide here at school, in the basement. Now, even though this is a test and for some reason Sister Rose Gertrude, your principal, decided to pull the alarm on the first day of school, in the very first hour of the new year, we must pretend it is real, so we will know what to do in case we are attacked. I have been assigned to take you down to the basement.

COLLEEN. You want me to get that sick, Sister?

SISTER MARY AGNES. No, Sister Mary Claire has a big heart, but a very weak stomach. She'll join us downstairs just as soon as she can. Put Jesus back in his spot, dear. Now, pick partners . . .

COLLEEN. Sister, how old are you?

SISTER MARY AGNES. Sixty six.

COLLEEN. Wow.

ELIZABETH. Sister, that's how old my grandmother is. Do you know her?

SISTER MARY AGNES. Follow me.

ELIZABETH. Lorretta Stokes.

SISTER MARY AGNES. Pleased to meet you.

(*All Exit, turn right, pass behind blackboard. Lights cross fade as they re-enter classroom through far* S.R. *door, into SISTER MARY LUCILLE's second grade classroom, 1963.*)

ELIZABETH. (*going over her lesson*) Honor thy mother and father. Honor thy mother and father. Honor thy mother and father.

SISTER MARY LUCILLE. (*Entering classroom*) Good morning, boys and girls.

ALL. (*not at all together*) Good morning, Sister Mary Lucille. Good morning, Sister Mary Lucille. Good morning, Sister Mary Lucille.

SISTER MARY LUCILLE. Saints preserve us. Second graders, if you find an air raid drill so exhausting, God help you when the real thing comes along. You've been running up and down from the basement for a year and a half. It's about time you developed some stamina. Second graders, take a crack at that word.

WANDA. (*raising her hand*) S-T-A-M-I-N-A. Stamina.

SISTER MARY LUCILLE. That's it. (*to all:*) . . . Boys and girls, it will take hard work to maintain the reputation that Catholic schools all over the country have earned. Please try to rise to the occasion or get out. (*pause*) Take your seats.

MARIA THERESA. (*to Wanda:*) Ask me. (*passes candy*) Here.

WANDA. (*taking candy*) What are the three kinds of sin?

MARIA THERESA. Number one, Original Sin: that is what you are born into. Number two, venial sin: that is when you tell a lie or do something that is not very nice to a stranger or your family. Number three, mortal sin: that is when you kill someone or knife them.

SISTER MARY LUCILLE. Second graders, please stop cramming and put those Baltimore Catechisms away. Donna Maria Gianetta, if you don't know it now, you never will. McHugh, stand up. Who made you?

ELIZABETH. (*standing*) God made me. (*SISTER MARY LUCILLE gestures and ELIZABETH stands.*)

SISTER MARY LUCILLE. Why did God make you?

ELIZABETH. God made me to feel this heart and when I'm all done with that to go back to his house in Heaven.

SISTER MARY AGNES. Where did you get that answer?

ELIZABETH. I asked God and He told me.

SISTER MARY AGNES. Don't you dare lie to me.

ELIZABETH. I'm not lying, Sister

SISTER MARY LUCILLE. Saints in heaven preserve us. Don't you dare stand in front of me and tell me that our Lord gave you that answer.

ELIZABETH. Sister that's what he said.

SISTER MARY LUCILLE. Well that's the wrong answer. Are you trying to tell me that God gave you the wrong answer? Because God is never wrong. Miss McHugh I don't know who you are talking to but it is not God. You will go home tonight and you will memorize the Baltimore Catechism or you will never receive the Body and Blood of Jesus Christ. Do you understand me? Sit down.

ELIZABETH. Yes, Sister. But I . . .

SISTER MARY LUCILLE. There will be no "buts" about it. Miss Sluska the seven sacraments in order.

WANDA. (*sing song*) Baptism, penance, First Holy Communion —

SISTER MARY LUCILLE. Louder. The boys in the back can't hear you.

WANDA. (*shouting*) Confirmation, Matrimony, Holy Orders, Extreme Unction.

SISTER MARY LUCILLE. Miss Sluska, very good. Miss Sluska, please thank your father for me and all the other sisters in the convent for his generous donation of roast beef for our Sunday dinner. There was not a line of gristle in that roast. He is fondly remembered in our morning prayers.

WANDA. Yes, Sister.

SISTER MARY LUCILLE. Miss Sluska is well on her way to making her first Holy Communion, which is more than I can say for a few select individuals in this classroom. Miss McHugh. Your parents are going to be in for the shock of their lives when all the other boys and girls are marching down the aisle to receive their first Holy Communion and you are not in line with them. Don't laugh, Mr. Crawford, a few of you are headed in the same direction. Now, let us stand and review what we will say when we go into the confessional for our first confession.

SISTER MARY LUCILLE.	GIRLS. (*bless themselves*) Bless me, Father, for I have sinned. This is my first confession.
(*blesses herself*) Bless me, Father, for I have sinned. This is my first confession.	

(*All except ELIZABETH kneel and stay frozen during the monologue.*)

ELIZABETH. Okay, everybody. This is church. This is God's house. If you ever have to talk to him just come right in and kneel down in one of these long chairs and start talking. But not too loud. ~~In here you have to be real quiet.~~ You might wake up the statues and they are praying to Jesus. (*bows her head*) Oh, I forgot to tell you something. Whenever you hear the name "Jesus" you have to bow your head or else you have a sin on your soul. Now, over there is the statue of Jesus' mother. Her name is The Blessed Virgin Mary. She is not as important as Jesus, so you don't have to bow your head when you hear her name. All the girls sit on her side when they go to mass. One time I heard that Margaret Mary O'Donahugue, a sixth grader, was in church saying the rosary, that's the necklace with beads on it for praying, she said that the Blessed Virgin Mary statue started crying right in the middle of Mass. I believe it, too. Sister says that there are miracles, magic things that happen to people that are real good. Margaret Mary never gets in trouble. In class she always gives the right answers, so I guess she deserves to see a miracle. Well, I'm going to get a miracle someday, too. Anyway, the boys sit on the other side of the church, the one with the statue of Saint Joseph. He is Jesus' father. (*bows head*) Hey, you forgot to bow your head. Don't do that cause you'll have a black spot on your soul and you'll go straight to hell. Now in hell it is real hot and you sweat a lot and little devils come and bite you all over. If you are real good you get to go to Heaven. In Heaven they have a big refrigerator full of stuff to eat. M and M's, ice cream, little chocolate covered doughnuts, anything you want to eat and it never runs out. But the best thing about Heaven is that you get to meet anyone you want. Let's say I wanted to meet Joan of Arc . . . no . . . no . . . Cleopatra. I would go to one of the saints and he would give me a permission slip and I would fill it out and give it to Jesus. (*bows head*) Hey, you didn't bow your head. Okay, I warned you. Then I would fly across Heaven, cause when you get in they give you wings, and I would have a chat with Cleopatra. The only thing is that I hope everyone I like gets accepted into Heaven or else I would never see them again. Jewish people can't go to Heaven. So if any of you are Jewish I would change into a Catholic or else you have to go straight to Hell. Jewish people can't even go to church. If I saw a Jewish person in church I would stand up and tell the priest that there was a Jewish person in church, and he would stop the Mass until they left. One time I heard this story and I know it is true, that a Jewish person went to church for two weeks disguised as a Catholic. He got communion every day except he took them out of his mouth so that they wouldn't melt and he put them in his kitchen cupboard so they would be safe. Then when he had gotten enough, thirteen or so, he put them in a frying pan and he cooked them and blood started dripping from the ceiling and it was Jesus' blood. (*bows head*) You see that crucifix up there. That's how Jesus died. The Jewish people put him up there and they killed him. If a Jewish person walked in here, that statue would turn bloody. Jesus would start hurting from the nails. That's all I wanted to say. I just wanted to tell you a few important things. I hope I haven't hurt anyone's feelings but that's just the way it is. Oh, one more thing, if you ask Jesus a question, make sure you write the answer down real fast, so you don't mess it up. 'Cause if you mess up an answer from him it could get you in real bad trouble.

(*Lights come back. Girls rise and assemble* U.S., *each pantomiming putting on communion veil. They talk until ready to form a line and Enter the "church" area.*)

COLLEEN. I'm starving. I can't wait to get hold of that host.

WANDA. That's disgusting, Colleen, and now you have a black spot on your soul and you can't receive.

COLLEEN. You believe anything.

WANDA. You thought about it. So that's a sin, too. You better get off this line or you'll have a mortal sin. (*They start walking into church.*)

COLLEEN. I don't care. I decided not to be a nun.

WANDA. You could change your mind again when you get into high school, and then what would happen? (*raising hand*) Besides, I'm telling.

COLLEEN. (*pushing her arm down*) No, you're not. Hey, look, your father. He's standing up to take your picture. You better smile.

ELIZABETH. Maria, look at Wanda's dress. It has these little sparkles all over it, it's pretty.

MARIA THERESA. I had to wear my sister's old dress. Look, it's ripped right here. My mother didn't even have time to sew it.

ELIZABETH. I have on my sister's, too. My grandmother couldn't come today but she gave me a little white rosary.

COLLEEN. My Aunt got me these new shoes. Hi, Aunt Dorothy. I have a white pocketbook with a silver dollar from my uncle in it.

MARIA THERESA. My father gave me this new watch. He almost had to go to work this morning but he's here. He's right there. (*She waves to him.*) Hi Daddy. He sees me. (*All have knelt except MARIA THERESA. ELIZABETH pulls her down. MARIA THERESA notices the priest approaching them.*) Hey, Father Moyhnihan is four away.

ELIZABETH. (*to COLLEEN:*) Four away. I can't wait.

COLLEEN. (*to WANDA:*) Four away.

WANDA. (*to imaginary person next to her*) Four away.

(They repeat in the same progression "three away," "two away," "one away." When the priest gets to MARIA THERESA; She sticks her tongue out to receive the host. She nudges COLLEEN and this pattern is repeated until completed. They end by crossing themselves.)

ELIZABETH. You guys, I bit the host.

MARIA THERESA. Which part? Maybe you bit off the arm of the baby Jesus.

ELIZABETH. You mean I have the arm of baby Jesus in my stomach. Oh, no.

MARIA THERESA. Uuch. It could be a leg.

WANDA. Elizabeth, you make me sick.

ELIZABETH. Jesus is dying inside of me. I feel it.

COLLEEN. Wanda your father is getting to me with that camera. Go stand somewhere else.

WANDA. Come on, Sister is calling our row.

ELIZABETH. Don't tell Wanda please.

(They rise and sing as they circle back into the classroom.)

ALL.
OH, HOW I LOVE JESUS.
OH, HOW I LOVE JESUS
OH, HOW I LOVE JESUS,
BECAUSE HE FIRST LOVED ME.

SISTER MARY LUCILLE. All right, class. You all looked beautiful on Saturday. That was one of God's small miracles, and I am glad to see you have the spirit of the Holy Ghost inside of you. I hope to see a marked improvement in your conduct from this day forward. Don't disappoint me or the Sacred Heart of Jesus or you will pay the consequences. (*passing out construction paper*) Now I would like you all to draw something to decorate the classroom for Thanksgiving. I will take ten minutes from my valuable class time. (*removing old decorations*) These Halloween decorations are a little passé. (*takes Mission Box from shelf*) Miss Russo, go around with the Mission Box. It's obvious you don't suffer for lack of food. I will be watching to see who puts how much in. Mr. Vaccaro, squeeze that pocket. I have eyes in the back of my head, or didn't you know that? They were put there by Jesus Christ himself. Now, perhaps some of my students have reflected over the weekend and have come up with some things that they are thankful for this year and I am sure they would like to share those thoughts with Sister Mary Lucille and the rest of the class. (*WANDA raises her hand.*) Yes, Miss Sluska, why don't you start? (*MARIA THERESA returns box to SISTER MARY LUCILLE.*) One minute. (*MARIA THERESA puts coin in box.*) This is a disgrace. (*Turns to crucifix and shakes box to show how little is in it, before replacing it.*) This is what the second grade in Yonkers, New York, has collected for you today. Sluska, go on.

WANDA. I am thankful that we have made our First Holy Communion this year and that we have a Catholic president.

SISTER MARY LUCILLE. An Irish Catholic President.

WANDA. Yes, Sister.

SISTER MARY LUCILLE. Very nice, Miss Sluska. Please remind your father that cameras and flashers do not belong in church. I do not like distractions during the consecration and thank him for that lovely leg of lamb.

WANDA. Yes, Sister.

SISTER MARY LUCILLE. Saints preserve us, Maria Theresa Russo. Don't suck your thumb in Sister Mary

Lucille's classroom. When your parents have a thousand dollars worth of orthodontist's bills to pay, I will be happy to tell them that you sat in my classroom, like a bump on a log, sucking your thumb. Your parents can't afford to take care of the nine children they have now, what kind of selfish daughter would expect them to pay for her bad habits in their later years? And tell your mother to scrub you down, you look like a stray cat. McHugh next. Keep that thumb out of your mouth. If you cannot control yourself, sit on your hands.

ELIZABETH. Was Jesus a Jewish person? Some kids I know said that our God, Jesus is Jewish.

SISTER MARY LUCILLE. In the two years you have been attending St. George's School, has there been any mention of Jesus, other than as a Catholic?

ELIZABETH. No, Sister, but I thought. . . .

SISTER MARY LUCILLE. You are not paid to think. Boys and girls, there is one thing, and only one thing to be aware about the Jews. They killed Jesus and that is the beginning and the end of it.

ELIZABETH. I am thankful for . . .

SISTER MARY LUCILLE. Hold on there, Miss Tish. Is that Cray-Pas on your desk? We use Crayola Crayons in this classroom. Don't we class?

ALL. Yes, Sister.

ELIZABETH. These are my grandmother's. She used to be an artist. She said if I was real careful, I could bring them to school and I could . . .

SISTER MARY LUCILLE. Class, Miss McHugh's grandmother is an artist.

ELIZABETH. No. She used to be.

MARIA THERESA. I know, Sister.

SISTER MARY LUCILLE. The class is not impressed.

Your grandmother is/was an artist, who cares? (*SISTER MARY LUCILLE takes Cray-Pas and throws it into the wastebasket. ELIZABETH sits at desk and begins to cry.*) No one told you to take that seat, young lady. I would like to know, as I am sure the whole class would, what you are thankful for this year?

ELIZABETH. (*trying to avoid looking at her*) I am thankful for . . .

SISTER MARY LUCILLE. Miss McHugh, you do not face the wall when Sister asks you a question. You face Sister.

ELIZABETH. I can't really be thankful for anything because the good things always turn bad.

SISTER MARY LUCILLE. Why do they turn bad?

ELIZABETH. Well, Sister, a lot of the time you make them turn bad.

SISTER MARY LUCILLE. Come here, Miss McHugh. (*ELIZABETH reluctantly crosses to teacher's desk.*) I joined the convent at thirteen years of age in the tradition of my country and my family and I began teaching when I was sixteen. I am now forty-seven years old. How many years have I been teaching, class?

WANDA. Thirty-one?

SISTER MARY LUCILLE. Right on the button. God willing I will be here for another thirty-one years, teaching long after you have gone. One day you will return and thank S̲ister for all she has done. Boys and girls, the sisters a̲re not here to be popular. We are here to teach you and to discipline (*pulls out ruler*) you, in spite of your bold and brazen ways. Miss McHugh, I have a personal message from me to you. In all my years of teaching, I have never met a spirit I couldn't break. Sometimes it takes one lesson and sometimes it takes one hundred.

(*Slaps ELIZABETH with ruler. Tapping is heard on the public address system.*) God, give me strength. Am I going to get any teaching done today?

VOICE ON THE P.A. SYSTEM. Boys and girls, this is your principal, Sister Rose Gertrude. I have a serious announcement to make and I hope you will cooperate by putting away what you are doing and listen carefully.

SISTER MARY LUCILLE. Fold your hands on top of your desks.

(*Lights dim slightly as news of President Kennedy's assassination is announced though not verbal. SISTER MARY LUCILLE rises, takes picture of Kennedy from bulletin board and places it under crucifix. This pantomime begins transition into fourth grade, 1965. ELIZABETH Exits to return as SISTER MARY THOMASINA. As lights come back up COLLEEN and MARIA THERESA are "twisting" D.S.R. in front of the teacher's desk.*)

MARIA THERESA. Show me again, how do they do it, Colleen?

COLLEEN. You're so dumb. Just copy me. Just like this.

MARIA THERESA. I'm not dumb, Colleen. Am I doing it right now?

COLLEEN. Hold out your hands and shake.

WANDA. Maria, it's like drying yourself with a towel.

COLLEEN. Who invited you, Miss Know-It-All? You stay out of here, Wanda.

MARIA THERESA. You could show me. Just a little, come on, Wanda.

COLLEEN. Maria, you're a little turncoat. Don't you dare listen to her, or I am not your friend.

WANDA. Colleen, I take dance classes.

COLLEEN. So what? Get out the book and show Maria the pictures.

WANDA. I didn't get the twist out of any book, Colleen.

COLLEEN. Yeah. Hey, if you think you're so great, why don't you just get up on that desk and show the whole class.

MARIA THERESA. Yeah, get up on the desk.

MARIA/COLLEEN. On the desk. On the desk. . . .

WANDA. Okay, okay, you guys. Watch Maria Theresa.

COLLEEN. If you look at her, I'll never talk to you again Maria. (*COLLEEN covers her eyes. MARIA watches.*)

MARIA THERESA I'm sorry, Colleen, but I've got to. Hey, you're good. Am I doing it right? It feels like it.

(*COLLEEN notices SISTER MARY THOMASINA by the doorway and sneaks back to her desk. MARIA THERESA notices too late, so does WANDA.*)

SISTER MARY THOMASINA. What are you doing by my desk?

MARIA THERESA. I left my book up here, Sister Mary Thomasina.

SISTER MARY THOMASINA. Are you in the habit of dropping things on my desk? Sit down. (*MARIA THERESA sits. WANDA has been trying to lower herself into her chair. SISTER MARY THOMASINA catches her mid-way down.*) No. Wanda. Don't you sit down, just yet. I would like you to go on with what you were doing. Go on, go ahead.

WANDA. It's just the twist, Sister.

SISTER MARY THOMASINA. Well, let's see it. (*WANDA twists again.*)

MARIA THERESA. She does it good, Sister.

SISTER MARY THOMASINA. So I see. (*COLLEEN laughs.*)

MARIA THERESA. She's better than you.

SISTER MARY THOMASINA. Colleen, if you think this is so funny, you may join her. No? I didn't think so. Now, girls, I don't think it is necessary to make a spectacle of yourselves, especially in front of the boys, do you, Wanda?

WANDA. No, Sister.

SISTER MARY THOMASINA. Wanda, get down. (*WANDA stands beside her desk. SISTER MARY THOMASINA writes SIN OF PRIDE on the blackboard.*)

SISTER MARY THOMASINA. There is a sin called the "sin of pride." It is when we call attention to ourselves or when we boast about our talents, that we are guilty of this sin. Now Wanda it is obvious that you are guilty of this vice, and that you need to develop a little humility. Until I see examples of humility accumulating in your character, I am going to have to strip you of your responsibility as fourth grade classroom monitor. Hand over your little book, please. (*WANDA takes off book, from around her neck, SISTER MARY THOMASINA hands it to COLLEEN.*) Colleen, you need help to develop a little responsibility. Let's see how you do.

WANDA. Are you going to tell my parents, Sister?

SISTER MARY THOMASINA. I see no reason to report to your parents . . . at least not at this point. You may be seated.

COLLEEN. Maria, aren't you going to congratulate me?

MARIA THERESA. I'm sorry, Wanda.

COLLEEN. Oh, you're just a sore loser.

SISTER MARY THOMASINA. All right. We have something to discuss. (*draws thermometer on blackboard*) Now as you all know, The Catholic Church is going through a fiscal crisis. If we cannot raise enough money this year to meet the cost of running the school, the government will come in here and we will be ordered to take down our statues and crosses and we will not be able to have any more religion classes. We could never mention God. We would be just like public school . . . For the past five years, my classroom has led in all areas of financial collection. Now Mr. McCarthy, Kevin's father, who is in the Knights of Columbus, has come up with an idea to raise money. The Knights of Columbus is going to sponsor a Talent Show. First prize will be twenty-five dollars. The boys have already come up with an idea and I think the girls could contribute some of their talents instead of wasting them during Sister's valuable class time.

WANDA. What are the boys doing, Sister?

SISTER MARY THOMASINA. The boys are going to do the Beatles. With the wigs and everything. Greg, stop tapping on that desk . . . I don't think we need a Ringo just yet.

COLLEEN. I've come up with an idea, Sister. Do you think we can have a few minutes to discuss it? Just a couple of us girls, in private?

SISTER MARY THOMASINA. That's the spirit, Colleen, but just a few minutes. The boys and the rest of you girls can use this time to clean out your desks. Frank, go around with the wastepaper pail.

(*The girls gather around COLLEEN's desk. Including*

ELIZABETH who "breaks" from SISTER MARY THOMASINA character.)

COLLEEN. Listen, I got a great idea. Why don't we do Diana Ross and The Supremes?

MARIA THERESA. Great idea. I can borrow my mother's high heels.

WANDA. Wait a second. I have a better idea. Why don't we all do Nancy Sinatra? Then we can wear white go-go boots. Besides, there are only three Supremes and there are four of us.

COLLEEN. You just go ahead and do Nancy Sinatra all by yourself. I don't want you in my act, got it? You're always trying to be different. Why don't you give it up, Polack?

ELIZABETH. It's not really a bad idea. If we do the Supremes we'd have to paint our faces black.

MARIA THERESA. No we wouldn't. Besides, the boys wouldn't recognize us.

COLLEEN. Look, who has the go-go boots, huh?

WANDA. I do.

COLLEEN. No kidding. Only child Polack gets everything she wants. Well, my mother won't get them for me.

MARIA THERESA. Mine either. And we would need them. I'm sorry, Wanda. Colleen, who is going to play Diana? I volunteer.

COLLEEN. I get to play Diana, it was my idea. I get to decide.

ELIZABETH. Colleen, you can't play Diana.

WANDA. I agree.

COLLEEN. Why?

WANDA. You are Irish and most of them have red hair and they look like "I Love Lucy." Everyone knows, Lucy can't sing and you can't either.

COLLEEN. What?

ELIZABETH. Maria does sing best.

COLLEEN. She can't dance.

WANDA. I'll help her. I know tap . . . almost. Maria, we'll make you into Diana. Let me see your skin.

MARIA THERESA. Wanda, I'll get Maria Rose to do the wash for me, she owes me. I'll be able to practice every day. I can't wait till my father sees me on that stage.

ELIZABETH. Let's take a vote. All for Maria as Diana, raise your hand. (*All raise hands except COLLEEN.*) Majority rules. Maria plays Diana.

COLLEEN. No. We will have a tryout and if I lose, which I won't, I still get to stand in front, got it!

ELIZABETH. Yeah, yeah.

WANDA. Let's go over to my house and rehearse after school.

COLLEEN. We'll go up to my room after school.

WANDA. I have a TV in my room and we can all watch "Dark Shadows."

COLLEEN. You better knock it off. You are showing off again. I'll tell Sister and she'll make you stop. I have her wrapped around my little finger and don't you forget it. She'll kick you right out of that talent show.

WANDA. Tell, I dare you.

COLLEEN. (*Raises her hand. All Exit as COLLEEN says following, except WANDA who stands in center.*) Sister, I think we have something to discuss. (*After all Exit WANDA begins.*)

WANDA. My father comes home from work every night and before he even takes off his gray hat with the skiny feather, he drops a bag of leaky, smelly meat on the table for my mother. She waits to see if she should kiss him or not. If it is just hamburger, she grunts. If it is liver, she practically goes to Mars. I hate liver. I hate all things sometimes. Even things I like. My ballet lessons, my pedal pushers, my dolls on the shelf, and I hate my smartness. You know why, because they were given to me. I am working on something that's mine. I have been for a long time. After school I go home and do my homework right away so I can go down to my father's store. He's not really a bad man, I just don't like him or something. While he is in the back room, sawing those bones out of the big legs of meat, I take soda cans and crush them onto my shoes. I move some sawdust into a little pile on the floor and I begin to dance. Not like Nancy Sinatra or Diana—oh, I am so much better. As I'm dancing, my mind just lets go and all these little movies come into my head. My favorite—I'm on the Ed Sullivan Show. (*mocks being handed a microphone*) Thank you, Eddie. I'm singing a song. Fake snow is falling all around me. I have on a sexy dress. It's sort of a sad song and I look so incredibly beautiful, that some people in the audience are starting to cry. Well, I break into a tap dance just to cheer them up. Later on Ed Sullivan brings me back stage to the Beatle's dressing room and Paul asks me to marry him. I say, maybe in a couple of months, because I have my career to think about. I become an international super-star and I go live in a penthouse apartment right on top of Radio City Music Hall. (*starts to put on go-go boots*) So for now I don't mind rehearsing in my father's store. He stays out of my way. I don't care if my hands and feet stick out a little too much, that can be fixed. I don't mind being Nancy Sinatra, I like these go-go boots a lot anyway. I made my mother buy them for me at S. Klien's. So here is DAWN GABOR, who used to be Wanda Sluska, coming to you live, right after eighth grade, to sing and dance, just because she feels like it. So you just get those TV sets warmed up, because even if it is a sin, I don't care, I'm going to be famous. Wait. Watch for me. Okay? (*WANDA does a baton twirling introduction to Diana Ross and the Supremes.*) I am happy to present, Sister Mary Thomasina's fourth grade class doing their rendition of "Stop In The Name of Love."

(*Scratchy version of song begins to play*. ELIZABETH and COLLEEN Enter followed by MARIA THERESA as Diana Ross. All wear feather boas. MARIA THERESA flirts with audience. COLLEEN tries to upstage her. WANDA tries to get into the act via her baton, streamers, and bubbles.*)
(*After finishing the number, straggle offstage, MARIA THERESA yanking COLLEEN off.*)

COLLEEN. Wait a minute, this was all my idea.

(*They circle back into the classroom, still wearing feather boas, WANDA twirling her baton. They Enter singing the theme song from a popular 1960's television "show".*)

COLLEEN. Maria, what happened to your father? He never showed up, did he?
WANDA. Shut up, Colleen.
COLLEEN. I'm talking to my ex-friend Maria, so butt out.
MARIA THERESA. My mother was there, he had to baby sit.

---

*Cautionary Note. Rights to produce the play do *not* include permission to use this song in production. For permission, producers must procure rights from *Stone Agate Music;* 6255 Sunset Blvd.; Los Angeles, CA 90028.

COLLEEN. Your mother had the baby with her, Maria.

MARIA THERESA. So what, Colleen, we have more than one baby, you know. I don't care about him anyway. Eddie saw me . . . He said I was great.

COLLEEN. Sure. Sure. (*SISTER MARY THOMASINA Enters.*)

SISTER MARY THOMASINA. Good morning, boys and girls.

ALL. Good morning, Sister Mary Thomasina.

SISTER MARY THOMASINA. I have a short announcement to make. Miss Carlson, the lay teacher in the eighth grade will be leaving us. She is getting married at the end of June.

COLLEEN. It's about time.

SISTER MARY THOMASINA. . . . and therefore a new teacher has been assigned. . . .

MARIA THERESA. I hope it is a guy.

SISTER MARY THOMASINA. Maria Theresa, it is certainly not a guy. Sister Mary Lucille will be moving up from the second grade. So there is a possibility that she will be seeing some old familiar faces in her class.

MARIA THERESA. Oh, God, yuuch.

SISTER MARY THOMASINA. Also, class, the talent show was an enormous success and we have the first prize winners, right here in class.

(*She looks from the boys to the girls while holding trophy and money. She moves toward girls. They cheer.*)

COLLEEN. I don't believe it.

MARIA THERESA. It was my Diana.

SISTER MARY THOMASINA. Let's hear a round of applause. Wanda, I liked your introduction.

WANDA. Thank you, Sister.

COLLEEN. Oh that was my idea, Sister.

SISTER MARY THOMASINA. Really, Colleen, I'm not surprised. Boys, it's too bad your wigs weren't on a little more securely. I'm sure you would have won second prize. Girls, I'm sure you want to be very generous and donate your prize earnings to the. . . .

COLLEEN. I have plans for this money.

SISTER MARY THOMASINA. . . . to the missions.

MARIA THERESA. I'll get the box.

(*MARIA THERESA gets the box and collects the money from COLLEEN. Then MARIA starts back to her seat.*)

SISTER MARY THOMASINA. The Knights of Columbus raised $256.75 on the little beer garden after the talent show. We are now in the 60th percentile. (*SISTER grabs MARIA THERESA's boa as she passes.*) And girls, please put those boas away. I think that there is a good chance, with our continued effort, that the school will be saved.

ALL. St. George's. St. George's. St. George's. (*WANDA twirls her baton.*)

SISTER MARY THOMASINA. Wanda. (*WANDA puts her baton in desk.*) Now, will you take out your math text books, please. Wanda, would you please pass these papers out so we may get started? (*WANDA passes paper to MARIA THERESA. MARIA hands WANDA a candy.*)

MARIA THERESA. Wanda, pssst, what's the answer to seven times seven?

SISTER MARY THOMASINA. No talking, boys and girls. Maria Theresa, are you having some sort of problem?

MARIA THERESA. Sister, I was just wondering, are we having a test?

SISTER MARY THOMASINA. This is not a test. This is your math homework for tonight. I would like it done neatly and signed by both your parents. And I would appreciate it, Maria Theresa, if you did not speak out in class. I would like to see your homework. Get it out. Quietly. (*WANDA returns from boy's side, clomping.*) Wanda, please stop clomping around the classroom like an elephant. And remove those go-boots. (*WANDA does so as SISTER MARY THOMASINA crosses to COLLEEN's desk.*) Colleen, your homework please. I don't believe I see a signature here. This homework is not signed.

COLLEEN. I told my parents to sign, Sister. The problem was that my dog had a heart attack and we had to take him to the hospital. So I guess my parents, just sort of forgot . . .

SISTER MARY THOMASINA. I want you to do this over, twenty-five times. I want you to have each copy signed by your parents. And Colleen, I don't want to see such negligence again. I do, however admire your imagination. Wanda your homework, please. Nice and neat and tidy. I wish all my students were as conscientious as you. 100%, Wanda. What's this ball point pen? We use Scheaffer fountain pens in the fourth grade. I don't like sneaks, Wanda. That will cost you, let's see . . . 85% that's fair.

WANDA. Sister, what about the Honor Roll?

SISTER MARY THOMASINA. Maria Theresa, your homework, please.

MARIA THERESA. (*Hands SISTER a torn and holey paper.*) I had to erase a little, Sister.

SISTER MARY THOMASINA. This is very messy. I told you if you could not erase completely to please make a new copy of your work. I know I did say this to the entire class. From now on I will no longer accept papers in this condition. This is not public school. Boys and girls, you will not get away with this here. If you want to go to public school, please take your books (*She piles everything in desk, on top of it.*) and messy papers and go down the street and go to public school. (*MARIA THERESA doesn't move.*) Fine. I didn't think so. Then do the work the way I want it done. I don't want to see dog-eared pages, no erasures, and if you must rip pages out of your notebook, please trim the edges before you come to class. (*A model airplane flies onto the floor.*) Bernard, does this belong to you? Oh, it does. Well, join it in the wastebasket. Now I would like to have a math quiz. Two volunteers come to the front of the classroom. I will ask the times tables. The winner will be allowed to skip the math homework and choose a holy card from Sister's own collection. Who would like to start? (*WANDA raises her hand.*) Let's have some new hands, for a change. (*COLLEEN raises her hand.*) What a pleasant surprise. Colleen come up front. Maria Theresa, how about you? I'm sure since you have such a difficult time with math you may want to have some fun with it. Come on, spit spot.

MARIA THERESA. Yes, Sister.

(*MARIA THERESA and COLLEEN stand by teacher's desk.*)

SISTER MARY THOMASINA. We will start with the easy ones. Maria Theresa, five times five?

MARIA THERESA. Twenty five.

SISTER MARY THOMASINA. Six times five?

COLLEEN. Thirty.

SISTER MARY THOMASINA. Four times four . . . Four times four?

MARIA THERESA. I thought you would call on us, four times four equals sixteen.

SISTER MARY THOMASINA. Maria Theresa, please do not repeat the question.

MARIA THERESA. It helps me to repeat the question.

SISTER MARY THOMASINA. Maria Theresa, we have been doing these times tables since the beginning of this year. I think you have had sufficient time to get them into your head, don't you agree?

MARIA THERESA. Yes, Sister.

SISTER MARY THOMASINA. Nine times six?

COLLEEN. Fifty-four.

SISTER MARY THOMASINA. Eight times eight? (*Pause. COLLEEN whispers answer to MARIA THERESA.*)

MARIA THERESA. Sixty-four.

SISTER MARY THOMASINA. Maria Theresa, did Colleen whisper that answer to you? Did I hear an answer whispered? I do not like that one bit. If you do not know an answer perhaps you should go stand in front of the blackboard and review your eight times tables. (*MARIA THERESA crosses D.S.R.*) Turn around and put your nose against that blackboard. (*MARIA THERESA places her nose against the blackboard so that she is facing front.*) The rest of the class is dismissed for lunch. Timothy, did you blow a bubble? Take that gum out of your mouth and place it on your nose and leave it there for the entire day. Colleen, I'd like a word with you privately. (*All Exit except MARIA THERESA who starts her monologue.*)

MARIA THERESA. Late at night when I'm lying in my bed, I ask myself some math questions and I get all the answers right. Then when I wake up and go to school and all the way there and all the way through religion class and on the line to go to the lavatory, the answers are still in my head. But just right before math class, they have fallen out of my brain when I wasn't thinking to hold them in. I am not stupid, even though my parents and

Sister think so. If we had math first thing, maybe they wouldn't go away. Sometimes, if my father comes home from work early, he helps me with my math homework. I don't want him to because if I give the wrong answer he gets mad and hits me. Usually my mother makes him stop but sometimes she is giving one of the babies a bath and she doesn't hear me. I think about math almost every single night. I can't help it. It makes me feel weird so I usually make a plan for a good happy dream so that when I do fall asleep I won't have a scary one. My favorite dream right now is that I live with someone else's family. Like I live with Donna Reed and I am the only child except that I have an older brother and sister. Donna Reed sends me to a school where there is no math or spelling. When I come home from school, my older brother takes me for a ride to the candy store in his yellow convertible. I make him put the top down and I sit in the back and my older sister combs my hair gently for a whole hour and lets me play with her make-up. Then we all get dressed up for dinner and we go downstairs. Donna Reed always cooks something real good for dinner. Stuff like steak or turkey with mashed potatoes and gravy. She never makes eggplant parmesan and tuna casserole. Dessert is always on the table so right after you finish your dinner you can just grab your dessert and eat it. Usually it is My-T-Fine chocolate pudding because Donna Reed knows that is my favorite. After the family is finished we are excused from the table and we go into the living room and everyone gathers around while I play the piano. Then my father, Mr. Reed, picks me up and carries me up the stairs to my room and tucks me into my very own canopy bed. He puts my stuffed animals around the bed so I will be safe and he leaves my Raggedy Ann and Andy night-light on so I won't be scared. Donna Reed kisses me on the forehead and tells me what a wonderful and beautiful daughter I am and how glad she is that she adopted me and I fall asleep. Sometimes I pray to Jesus about something. Jesus tells me not to think that my parents don't love me. He says that they will probably not get mad at me if I bring home another bad mark in math and spelling. So I believe him, but something always happens when I get home anyway.

(*ELIZABETH Enters.*)

ELIZABETH. Maria, she's gone. (*MARIA THERESA doesn't respond.*) Maria, she went to the convent to have lunch, come on.

MARIA THERESA. Elizabeth, do you think it is a sin to pray to Jesus and ask Him to kill certain people in a car crash?

ELIZABETH. Yes, I think so. But I think you can pray and ask Him to send them to a hospital for a little while. I don't think that counts as a sin.

MARIA THERESA. Okay, repeat after me . . . "Dear Jesus . . ."

ELIZABETH. Maria Theresa, this is your prayer, I don't have to say it.

MARIA THERESA. But if two people say it, He is going to listen harder, maybe. Please.

ELIZABETH. . . . "Dear Jesus . . ."

MARIA THERESA. Please send Sister Mary Thomasina . . .

ELIZABETH. (*crossing her fingers*) Please send Sister Mary Thomasina . . .

MARIA THERESA. and my whole family . . . especially my father . . .

ELIZABETH. (*crossing her feet*) and my whole family . . . especially my father . . ."

MARIA THERESA. To Saint Bernadette's Hospital . . .

ELIZABETH. To Saint Bernadette's Hospital . . . Amen."

MARIA THERESA. I didn't say Amen yet. ". . . at least until I graduate from eighth grade. Thank you very much, signed Maria Theresa Russo, fourth grade, Saint George's School, Yonkers, New York. Amen."

ELIZABETH. ". . . at least until I graduate from eighth grade. Thank you very much. Maria Ther . . . (*MARIA THERESA nudges her.*) Elizabeth, fourth grade, Saint George's School. Amen."

MARIA THERESA. You have to say your last name.

ELIZABETH. McHugh. Elizabeth McHugh.

MARIA THERESA. Okay, great. Elizabeth, you are my very best friend. Let's go eat. (*starts out of room*)

ELIZABETH. (*calling after her*) Wait for me outside, I forgot my Chinese jumprope.

MARIA THERESA. (*Exiting*) Okay, hurry.

ELIZABETH. (*races back to where she stood for prayer*) Jesus, this is Elizabeth, Elizabeth McHugh, fourth grade, Saint George's School. Please forget everything I just said about the hospital and everything. I was only kidding and besides I had my fingers crossed just in case you didn't notice. Please don't forget to take my name off the list. Thank you very much. I'm sorry we haven't been talking that much lately. Listen, can I ask you something? A couple of us girls were wondering, are you Jewish? Let me know as soon as you can, okay? I love you, Elizabeth.

(*Starts to Exit, then runs back, genuflects and Exits as the lights dim.*)

END OF ACT I

ACT II

Patti Smith's "Gloria"* is playing as the curtain rises. GIRLS Enter as if returning from lunch. They Enter the lavatory and ELIZABETH, COLLEEN and MARIA THERESA begin to groom themselves. WANDA prepares her "experiment" and when she is ready she signals the girls to watch. She has a tampon which she unwraps, dunks in a glass of water and as it expands, All squeal and giggle with delight. COLLEEN grabs it away from WANDA and threatening MARIA THERESA, chases her out of the lavatory, down the hall and into the classroom. WANDA is in hot pursuit. Sixth grade, 1967.

WANDA. (*at classroom doorway, grabs tampon*) Colleen, you make me sick. Put that thing away. Someone will see it, the boys or something.

COLLEEN. Wanda, my brothers see these all the time. No big deal about it.

WANDA. Really. I don't think my father knows about it.

COLLEEN. God, he's got to know about it.

WANDA. Hey, Colleen how come Maria's not in school today?

COLLEEN. Mr. Russo is in jail.

WANDA. What?

COLLEEN. It's true. I swear. My mother told me. Somebody pushed him out of line in the A and P. And he hit the guy on the head with a can of grapefruit juice.

---

*Cautionary Note: Permission to produce this play does not include permission to use this music in productions. Producers must procure rights from the copyright owner.

38

WANDA. Really?

COLLEEN. Yeah, the cops came and everything. The whole family went to pick him up this morning. My mother told me I can't go over to Maria's house anymore, but I think I can still talk to her in school.

ELIZABETH. (*Entering*) Hey, you guys, guess what?

COLLEEN. Thanks for calling me back last night, Elizabeth.

ELIZABETH. I'm sorry. My house was nuts last night. But I've got great news, my grandmother is moving in next week.

COLLEEN. Great.

WANDA. Is everyone excited?

ELIZABETH. No. No one wants her but me. She's going in my room. Mary Pat is moving into the living room. I can't wait.

COLLEEN. Good luck.

ELIZABETH. Why?

WANDA. Watch out, Colleen's turning green.

ELIZABETH. Why, what's the matter?

COLLEEN. Just that when my grandmother moved in with us everything got creepy. She was always complaining. And she even had her own room. I wouldn't sleep with her.

ELIZABETH. Why not?

COLLEEN. 'Cause she could just die right there while I was sleeping.

ELIZABETH. My grandmother wouldn't die on me, Colleen.

COLLEEN. (*reading from* True Confessions) "It was just a little game but we didn't know all the rules. He only did it half way, yet I got pregnant. God help me if Momma finds out who I played with."

WANDA. Let me see that. "Nightmare in the

Classroom." "They stripped me naked just for kicks while so many hands and lips did dirty things to me." Wooooh, Colleen, where did you get this?

COLLEEN. From my baby-sitting house. They have *Playboy* too. And she, the lady, has those little birth control pills.

WANDA. She's not a Catholic.

COLLEEN. No kidding.

ELIZABETH. Could I see that?

COLLEEN. No, get your grandmother to show you. Wanda, look at this.

WANDA. How do they fit together like that?

ELIZABETH. Wait a minute. My grandmother may be coming to live with us but we're still best friends, I swear. She's sick and she can't move around too much for awhile. So after school I may go home to see her, but that's it.

COLLEEN. What about basketball?

ELIZABETH. I can still go. Come on. I'm not a flat leaver. (*grabs magazine*) Page 45, a sexy word quiz. "A fun fill-in puzzle for women who know the language of loving." 14 down. Sixty-nine. Wanda, what does sixty-nine mean? I heard you knew.

WANDA. Get lost.

COLLEEN. I happen to know what it means. It means the guy's thing is six inches long and in nine months you have a baby.

ELIZABETH. That's not it.

COLLEEN. Or that he sticks it in you and in nine months you have a six-inch baby.

ELIZABETH. That answer has too many letters.

COLLEEN. You're right.

ELIZABETH. After school we'll go to the library and look it up.

COLLEEN. Wanda, you're not invited.

SISTER MARY GERMAINE. (*Entering*) Good afternoon, boys and girls.

ALL. Good afternoon, Sister Mary Germaine.

SISTER MARY GERMAINE. You may all be seated. Now Colleen has a little announcement to make (*WANDA raises hand.*) Yes, Wanda.

WANDA. Sister, I have an announcement about cheerleading.

COLLEEN. Copy cat.

SISTER MARY GERMAINE. We'll hear about that tomorrow, thank you, Wanda.

COLLEEN. Ha.

SISTER MARY GERMAINE. Boys, file quietly to the back one by one and remove your sneakers and things from the cloakroom for physical fitness. Row one, Francis, you may start. Go on, Colleen.

COLLEEN. Saturday afternoon at 1:30 Father Moyhnihan is going to unlock St. Steven's auditorium and all the girls are going to meet for the first round of basketball tryouts. Sister Mary Redemptor will show us what we need to know. But I happen to know a few "secret" plays. Pick and roll, and split the post, which I can show to a couple of the girls. My brothers taught them to me. Boys' basketball is different from girls' basketball but we can still use these plays because they don't look too rough even though they really are. My brother T.J. (*A look from SISTER MARY GERMAINE.*) Thomas James, says "it's not the strength, it's the skill," and he should know because he plays for Iona College. (*WANDA is making faces to distract COLLEEN.*) Now don't forget sneakers so that you won't scratch the gym floor. Oh, and bring some shorts so that you can jump real high and still be modest. And no chewing gum . . .

SISTER MARY GERMAINE. Colleen, is there something the matter?

COLLEEN. Yes, Sister, Wanda is trying to make me laugh.

WANDA. I was not.

COLLEEN. Was too.

WANDA. Was not.

SISTER MARY GERMAINE. Wanda, cut it out. Please. Try to practice some self control. Russell, check that fly!

WANDA. Did you see it?

ELIZABETH. I think I saw a little pink.

COLLEEN.   . . . gum chewing because it could go right down your throat and strangle you. Oh, and this year we are going to get new uniforms, better than the cheerleaders.

WANDA. I doubt it.

COLLEEN. Fact of life.

SISTER MARY GERMAINE. Colleen, wrap it up, please.

COLLEEN. Yes, Sister. And it is good for school spirit and the church gets to make a lot of money because it costs fifty cents a head to get in.

WANDA. Who's going to pay to see a bunch of girls, huh?

ELIZABETH. When we start winning, they'll be busting down the doors.

COLLEEN. That's right. That's all for today, Sister.

SISTER MARY GERMAINE. That was very nice public speaking, Colleen, you may be seated. Now, boys, are you all packed up? Good. File down to the gym. I don't want to hear a single sound on that line. Terrence, take names. Now, who are the two girls who will report to us today? (*WANDA and COLLEEN raise their hands.*) Now last week we were discussing puberty during health class . . . acne, fried foods, regular bathing.

WANDA. Yeah, until Richard Krause busted right in the classroom, without knocking.

COLLEEN. Dick Krause.

SISTER MARY GERMAINE. . . . deodorants, etc. Now, today, girls, the assignment was to consult the "Little Pictorial Lives of the Saints" and report back to the class on what you found particularly relevant under the title Saint So-and-So, Virgin, comma, martyr. Then, right after these two reports, we will have another brief discussion on personal hygiene. Which one of you would like to start? (*WANDA raises her hand.*)

WANDA. (*crossing to in front of teacher's desk*) January 21st, Saint Agnes, Virgin, Martyr.

SISTER MARY GERMAINE. Sister Agnes' patron saint, yes, Wanda, go on.

COLLEEN. Brown nose.

WANDA. St. Agnes, virgin, martyr, was 12 years old when she was led to the altar and was commanded to offer incense which was part of the rules in Rome at the time. She didn't want to offer incense because it was against her religion, so instead, she raised her hand to Jesus, and made the sign of the cross. The King got really mad when he saw . . .

SISTER MARY GERMAINE. People get mad, dogs get angry.

WANDA. Yes, Sister. The King got really angry when he saw this and he had her tied up but the bandages would not stay on and so he made her take off all her clothes and stand in front of the pagan crowd. But nobody could see her because Jesus performed a miracle and made a blinding light appear so everyone had to look away. One person, a guy, did not turn away because he wanted to see St. Agnes naked. But the light made him blind and he had to be carried away. The King was really mad—angry now and he had a death sentence passed and he had St. Agnes' head chopped off in one blow. Just before she died she managed to say, "Christ is my spouse. He chose me first and His will be done." After she died the angels came to get her body and took it straight to Heaven.

SISTER MARY GERMAINE. Now, Wanda, in your own words, can you tell the class what that story means to you?

WANDA. Well, that saint made up her mind that she wanted to follow Jesus and nothing was going to tempt her.

SISTER MARY GERMAINE. The Saint also represents youth. After all she was only 12 years old. It illustrates how hard you must try to keep your innocence, doesn't it, class?

ALL. Yes, Sister.

SISTER MARY GERMAINE. Also the part of the story we haven't discussed, was when the young man was blinded as he tried to gaze at the body of the young Saint. Now, girls, God protected St. Agnes from this man and even though God is all-knowing, He can't be in all places at all times. You must take some responsibility yourselves. Now I have something for you girls. Wanda please come up to my desk and pass these out. Girls these are some sanitary napkin kits for you to take home. They were donated by Mr. Lorenzo. He has asked me to remind you to tell your parents that all members of our parish are eligible for a 10 per cent discount. So please patronize his store. Take these home and show them to your mothers. They will explain.

COLLEEN. My mother explained it already. (*WANDA looks in bag.*)

SISTER MARY GERMAINE. Please do not be gazing at

those things here in my classroom. There is a proper place and time for everything. Girls, all eyes up here. You are at the age where you are beginning to provoke the boys. I don't want to see legs crossed in my classroom and I don't want to see uniform skirts that are shorter than regulation length. As a matter of fact let me check them now. (*girls kneel*) Elizabeth, when was the last time you took an iron to that skirt? That skirt is too short, Colleen. Take it down two inches by tomorrow. Wanda, perfect.

WANDA. I iron my own uniform blouses.

SISTER MARY GERMAINE. All right back to your seats. (*WANDA raises hand.*) Yes, Wanda.

WANDA. (*About something in bag.*) Sister, I was just wondering what's this for?

COLLEEN. Oh, brother.

SISTER MARY GERMAINE. Wanda, ask your mother. Colleen, let's hear from you. Nice and loud and clear.

COLLEEN. (*crossing to teacher's desk*) I have Saint Agatha, virgin, martyr, February 5th. She was from Sicily.

SISTER MARY GERMAINE. Which is in Italy.

COLLEEN. And she was going to be Jesus' spouse, too. A judge sent for her when he heard how pretty and how rich she was. So she went because he made it into a law but she asked Jesus to help her not be harmed by him. When she got there she was thrown in jail because she refused to fall into sin with him. She was locked into a cell until she could change her mind. She didn't change her mind so the judge got real angry and started to torture her. The next thing he did was to strip her of her clothes and send her to a place where the sheep were. Then he took one of her breasts and cut it off. (*starts to laugh*) And then Jesus heard her scream and sent one of the apostles to put it back on. (*laughs some more*) And then Jesus accepted her prayer of wanting to join him in Heaven so he ended her life and took her to Heaven. (*composing herself*) I'm sorry.

SISTER MARY GERMAINE. Sorry or not, Colleen, I have a few important things to say to you. The life of a saint is a very important and holy thing and I will not have that life mocked at in my classroom. It is sacrilegious and perhaps even a sin, I will check into that. Second, Colleen, and I want all the girls to listen closely to this because it concerns some of you. I have been keeping an eye on you and I am sorry to say that you are going right down the drain.

COLLEEN. Sister, I am not.

SISTER MARY GERMAINE. You might be dragging some of your friends down with you. There is a type of girl that gets into trouble, that gets a bad reputation. Colleen, stand over by that blackboard. Face us. Now, girls, looking at Colleen you may not be able to tell from her outward appearance that her soul has turned black and shriveled up smaller and smaller, so that it has almost entirely disappeared . . .

ELIZABETH. I disagree.

SISTER MARY GERMAINE. And who are you to disagree, Elizabeth? What kind of girl might choose Colleen for a friend or even an aquaintance? I would venture to guess and say someone who has a soul in the same sad condition.

ELIZABETH. You can't see Colleen's soul.

SISTER MARY GERMAINE. Elizabeth, take yourself for a little walk down to the principal's office.

ELIZABETH. What should I say to her?

SISTER MARY GERMAINE. Tell her you are doubting

the word of Sister Mary Germaine and the Catholic church.

ELIZABETH.	COLLEEN.
Yes, Sister.	Score one for their side.

(*ELIZABETH Exits.*)

SISTER MARY GERMAINE. Enough said. You can use the rest of the time to clean your desks and get your own gear ready for physical fitness. Monica, go around with the waste basket.

(*Lights down except for COLLEEN monologue spot.*)

COLLEEN. I used to go out with this guy, Ricky. I liked him a lot for awhile. We hung around Cross County Shopping Center on Saturdays. We used to get red pistachio nuts and then we'd wait till our hands got all red and sweaty. Then we'd go upstairs on the escalator to the Wedding Shop and smear all the white dresses with our hands. It looked like The Bride of Frankenstein, I swear. One time we went to the movies on a Friday night. Me and Ricky saw "Born Free." It was okay for awhile but then toward the end it got bad. The girl lion gets killed and it's really sad. I started to cry even, but I didn't let that Ricky see. I hate to let a boy see me cry. The day we broke up, Ricky and me were sitting in the back of his father's car in the garage. He gave me his ID bracelet and then he tried to put his hand somewhere. I ran right out of that car but I kept the bracelet just for spite. I told my mother about it. Me and my mother are just like this. (*holds two fingers together.*) She told me I did the right thing. Then she started giving me a speech about sex stuff. She told me about the change and how it was part of becoming a woman. She told me when I got it, it would be such a happy day that we would go out to lunch and have a party all day long. Just me and her. Ha. I don't want to be a woman. I like myself the way I am. My chest is growing, and I think there is hair coming out of, you know, down there. Well anyway, Sister told everyone to finish up with their desks and to pack up. I felt something. I tried to close my legs so it would stop. I held my stomach in, real hard, but it kept leaking. I didn't know the whole thing was so messy. I didn't want to move. I took my sweater off and I wrapped it around me. I knew what it was. After Monica put the wastebasket back, Sister Mary Germaine told me to take my seat. But even before I started to move, she asked me about my sweater. She thought I was trying to show off with sex or something, I guess. She said, "Take that sweater off, it's seventy degrees in this classroom." My stomach hurts, it makes me feel better." "I'll ask you one more time, take it off." The boys began to come into the classroom, she didn't care, she let them. I couldn't look at her. She hit me. I put my hands to my face and she ripped the sweater off, digging her nails into my side. I just stood there against the blackboard. Everyone was looking at me. Then she made an announcement to the class, that in all her years of teaching, she had never come across someone with such a lack of concern for their personal hygiene. She said these things right in front of the boys. I thought I was going to die. A couple of drops of blood got on the floor. She made one of the boys go down to the janitor's closet and get a mop. The nurse came in and took me out of class. I never want to go back there again. She is trying to make me feel guilty. I do feel guilty. I am a jerk. I wish I was dead, and never had to see you or anybody else again. I wish I had never become a woman. I'm no good at it. Is that what you wanted to hear, Sister? All right, I'm no good at it.

(*COLLEEN Exits. Lights return. Eighth grade, 1969. MARIA THERESA has a transistor radio, plugged into her ear. We hear a 1960's type ballad playing. ELIZABETH has been rumaging through her purse, as they Enter.*)

MARIA THERESA. Elizabeth, hi. I missed you soooo much. How was your summer?

ELIZABETH. It was great . . . except my grandmother had another heart attack.

MARIA THERESA. Oh, no.

ELIZABETH. She's better now. Hey did you see those guys walk on the moon?

MARIA THERESA. Nah, I fell asleep.

ELIZABETH. It was neat. I was scared, for a minute. You know, Maria, they made up that, "one giant step . . ." slogan, months before. Rip off. (*COLLEEN Enters wearing sunglasses.*)

COLLEEN. Hey you guys.

MARIA THERESA. I got your postcard. "Wish you were here." Ha ha.

COLLEEN. I wanted to bring back an alligator pocketbook, but my mother said it was too ugly. We don't get along like we used to. She's getting crazy. My brothers and I palled around mostly. All the guys down there thought I was in high school, I swear.

MARIA THERESA. Big deal.

COLLEEN. Let me see that. (*puts radio plug in her ear*)

MARIA THERESA. My father got it for me.

COLLEEN. It isn't your birthday till December.

MARIA THERESA. He bought us all presents because he threw the dining room table against the wall, one Sunday during breakfast. Everyone got real upset. Eggs were hanging off the wall.

COLLEEN. He's nuts.

MARIA THERESA. No, he's not.

ELIZABETH. Hey, did you see Wanda? She's got these cool aviator glasses. She wears them just like Gloria Steinem.

COLLEEN. Who?

MARIA THERESA. The women's libber.

COLLEEN. They're crazy. My father says, watch out if a girl becomes president.

ELIZABETH. How come?

COLLEEN. They could get the curse in the middle of something and cause World War Three.

ELIZABETH. I'm glad we didn't get Lucy for home-room. Do you think she'll recognize us?

MARIA THERESA. How could she forget? Maria Theresa says, Agie is great, though. She says Agie's got one foot in the grave.

(*SISTER MARY AGNES Enters. She is carrying a shopping bag and sprinkles holy water on the class and room as she Enters.*)

SISTER MARY AGNES. Good morning, boys and girls.

ELIZABETH. Steady girl.

MARIA THERESA. Sister, watch my hair please.

SISTER MARY AGNES. Good morning, boys and girls.

ALL. Good morning, Sister Mary Agnes.

COLLEEN. Didn't we do this already?

MARIA THERESA. She forgets things, and I think she's

gotten worse. (*SISTER MARY AGNES writes her name on the black board.*)

SISTER MARY AGNES. Sister — Mary — Agnes.

COLLEEN. We heard, Agie.

SISTER MARY AGNES. Would two of you children come up here and pass these out? This will be a very big year for you eighth graders. We have a great deal to discuss. Now this year you will be graduating . . .

MARIA THERESA. Are we going to have a boy/girl dance?

| MARIA THERESA. I have a dress, all picked out. It's lay-away. Wait till you see it. | SISTER MARY AGNES. In spite of that punch being spiked last year . . . |

SISTER MARY AGNES . . . there will be an eighth grade dance. Sister Mary Lucille will be handling the details. Oh, and we have to discuss the co-ops.

| SISTER MARY AGNES. Now at my first dance, I had the prettiest dress. White, of course, with small pearls around my neck. My mother was a seamstress. She made all my things. My brother, Jed, played the piano. I loved that dress. I had a lovely time, too. Rufus Quinn brought me a small bouquet of lilies of the valley, with a lilac ribbon around them. Rufus had some scent on too. He smelled so nice: like wood. | COLLEEN. It was so long ago, she probably danced with a brontosaurus rex.

ELIZABETH. When are the co-ops, Sister? That's our ticket out of here?

COLLEEN. So what did your mother do?

MARIA THERESA. When? Do you like my hair like this?

COLLEEN. Put it over more. Hold it. When your father went nuts.

MARIA THERESA. She just went into the kitchen and did the dishes. |

After the dance, we had a snack. Shortenin' bread and milk with a little taste of honey in it . . . Oh, and then we sang a hymn. (*begins to hum song*) "Ah humm . . . I need thee, precious Jesus, for I am filled with. . . . filled with?

COLLEEN. I wouldn't take that.

ELIZABETH. Me neither. I'm never getting married.

MARIA THERESA. They might get a divorce.

ELIZABETH. What?

COLLEEN. Maria's parents are getting a divorce.

MARIA THERESA. God, don't announce it. I swear, I hope they do. Mind your own business, Anselm.

COLLEEN. Who would you go live with?

ELIZABETH. Maria, you'll still be in high school with us, right? Oh, it would be the worst if we couldn't all stay together. What about open house about St. Mary's? What about the co-ops?

MARIA THERESA. Hey, Sister, I'm not singing any hymns at that dance.

COLLEEN. She can't hear you, watch this. (*COLLEEN drops books on the floor with a loud bang.*)

ELIZABETH. Is she ever going to get to the co-ops?

SISTER MARY AGNES. Oh, look, you dropped your books, dear. Now what was that song? Rufus had a good strong voice, didn't you, dear? Oh, yes . . ." I need thee precious Jesus, for I am filled with . . .

COLLEEN. Filled with what, spit it out?

SISTER MARY AGNES. "Filled with . . . sin," thanks

Rufus. (*Girls applaud*) Oh and after we sang that hymn, I bent back my head and Rufus kissed me, right like that.

MARIA THERESA. She actually made out with a guy?

ELIZABETH. What do you think she used to look like?

MARIA THERESA. A dog.

COLLEEN. Sister have any of the other nuns made out with guys? What about Sister Mary Germaine?

MARIA THERESA. Another Bow Wow Club member.

SISTER MARY AGNES. Oh, yes, dear, Sister Mary Germaine was quite a looker in her day. I have seen pictures.

COLLEEN. I'd love to get my hands on those negatives.

MARIA THERESA. Sister, what happened to Rufus, is he a priest or something?

COLLEEN. He ditched her.

SISTER MARY AGNES. After high school, he enlisted in the Army. He was blown up.

MARIA THERESA. Yuuch.

ELIZABETH. So you had to join the convent?

SISTER MARY AGNES. I didn't have to join the convent. I wanted to. I had another beau after Rufus. We used to take long walks, arm in arm, around the trails of West Point.

ELIZABETH. Sometimes, I don't think God knows what He is doing.

SISTER MARY AGNES. God always knows what He is doing, Loretta.

ELIZABETH. Sister, my name is Elizabeth.

COLLEEN. She called you by your grandmother's name. She's spooky.

SISTER MARY AGNES. Did someone have a question?

MARIA THERESA. She's a witch. A nun-witch. Look at that nose real close . . .

SISTER MARY AGNES. No questions, good let's move on.

ELIZABETH. Sister, I have a question, the co-ops?

SISTER MARY AGNES. The results come in the mail. The children just line up by that phone in the hallway and the noise is . . . well, I tell them that patience is a virtue, but you can't tell children anything these days. The co-ops are the entrance exams you must take if you want to get into Catholic high school. Did we do this already? When you are as old as I am, one year just blends into the next.

COLLEEN. No, Sister.

SISTER MARY AGNES. Thank you, dear. Now I will be teaching math and current events and . . . something else . . . well, don't worry it will be come back to me, it always does. Lucille will be teaching English and science in the class across the hall.

COLLEEN. I love Lucy.

MARIA THERESA. (*trying to read handwriting in SISTER MARY AGNES' book which was left on her desk*) Look at the way she spells co-ops. March 5th. I can't read her writing.

SISTER MARY AGNES. Dear, is there something the matter with your eyes? That says Blessed Sacrament High School. You should get those bangs cut. What was your name, Mary Alice?

MARIA THERESA. Maria Theresa.

SISTER MARY AGNES. Well, Mary Thomas, don't you think you should get those bangs cut? I remember a story about a young lady who had a hair-do she liked so much . . . I believe you would call it a beehive. How can you see from behind all that hair? Well, she never washed her hair because she didn't want to ruin it. About two months later, she went to the doctor's . . . Eugene, could you please stop shaking him? Thank you . . .

MARIA THERESA. What happened to the girl with the beehive?

SISTER MARY AGNES. Who? . . . oh . . . yes. Well, when she went to the doctor's he found bugs all in her hair and they were eating her brains out. Now we all want to see your pretty face, don't we, dear?

COLLEEN. Yeah, we all want to see her pretty face, don't we, Eddie?

MARIA THERESA. Drop dead. I think it's time to change classes, Sister.

SISTER MARY AGNES. Thank you dear. Let me check.

ELIZABETH. Sister, are you looking for something? Are you looking for your glasses?

SISTER MARY AGNES. I know I put them somewhere . . . now, just one second . . .

ELIZABETH. Sister, they are around your neck.

SISTER MARY AGNES. So they are. I put them there so I wouldn't forget them. Isn't that funny?

MARIA THERESA. Hysterical, we're all dying. Let me out of here.

SISTER MARY AGNES. It *is* time to change classes. Would you like me to walk you?

COLLEEN. No. It's right across the hall. Hey, Sister, thanks again. (*COLLEEN and MARIA THERESA Exit.*)

SISTER MARY AGNES. Have a nice afternoon. Good bye, Loretta.

ELIZABETH. I said my name is Elizabeth.

SISTER MARY AGNES. (*ignoring her and singing*) I need, precious Jesus . . . (*ELIZABETH looks at her and Exits.*) Rufus, there is one thing I have been meaning to . . .

(*SISTER MARY AGNES Exits. The girls circle around and change to SISTER MARY LUCILLE's classroom.*)

MARIA THERESA. Wanda, did you ever show up at Saint Mary's open house yesterday?

WANDA. Yeah. I was in the science lab for most of it. Maria, we get to disect frogs in sophmore year.

MARIA THERESA. Oh.

WANDA. The science teacher showed me these little dead mice in jars. It was really neat.

MARIA THERESA. Well, I didn't brown nose with any teachers. I was in the cafeteria. You got to check out that food. Every Wednesday, they have little fried chicken wings with gravy and lasagna.

ELIZABETH. Did you see the principal? She's real young. She doesn't wear a habit. That place is perfect.

MARIA THERESA. What if I don't get in?

WANDA. You'll get on the waiting list, at least. Don't worry. (*SISTER MARY LUCILLE Enters.*)

SISTER MARY LUCILLE. Sit down. How many times do I have to tell you I don't want to hear any stressing or laughing in that hallway? I will just sit back and see who gets into Catholic high school and who doesn't. I have left students back in the eighth grade and I will do it again. Watch your P's and Q's. Now, business at hand. In three short weeks the archdiocese of New York will hold the Seventh Annual forensic Tournament. Six students have submitted speeches on the theme for this year, "Outstanding Current World Leaders." Mr. Farrell and Miss Howes, your marks are not satisfactory. I want my class to capture that First Prize trophy — fourth year in a row. Mr. Mackenzie, your lisp, while I admire your determination, disqualifies you. Mr. Egan, "Selected Works of Archbishop Fulton Sheen," approved and good luck. And finally, Wanda Sluska — "The Inaugural Address of our Late Great John Fitzgerald Kennedy," wise choice, Miss Sluska. (*ELIZABETH raises hand.*)

Between your elocution and style, Jack Kennedy's words, and my careful coaching, God will surely be on our side. First prize is . . . Yes, Miss McHugh, what is it?

ELIZABETH. Sister, I submitted a speech. I was wondering . . .

SISTER MARY LUCILLE. I was coming to that, Miss McHugh. Patience is a virtue. Miss Sluska, good luck. Miss McHugh I have rejected your speech.

ELIZABETH. Sister, it's under eight minutes. I timed it twice.

SISTER MARY LUCILLE. I have no quarrel with the length, Miss McHugh, it is the subject matter. In all good conscience, I cannot allow a student in my classroom to enter the Seventh Annual Forensic Tournament with the words of a non-Catholic.

ELIZABETH. But he *was* a Christian.

SISTER MARY LUCILLE. "I Have a Dream" by Martin Luther King Jr., leave it to the public schools. Who exactly did Martin Luther King lead anyway? Miss McHugh pick another speech. From a Roman Catholic author, this time. Perhaps you should look at the words of Pope John the XXIII, his work in the ecumenical council. No more Latin Mass. Guitars. Dialogue with other faiths. Right up your alley.

ELIZABETH. But I prepared—there isn't enough time to choose a new. . . .

SISTER MARY LUCILLE. End of discussion. We have three and a half minutes to spend on the dance, no more, no less. (*ELIZABETH throws a note to WANDA.*) You are very bold and brazen, who do you think you are?

WANDA. Nobody, Sister.

SISTER MARY LUCILLE. Well, Miss Nobody, hand Sister that note. (*She reads the note and crumples it.*)

Miss McHugh, if you expect me to be shocked and annoyed at your behavior, you are going to have to do a lot better than this. Grow up, Miss McHugh, and find stronger ammunition if you want to tangle with me. Take the seat furthest away from me and sit there for the remainder of the year. Do you understand me?

ELIZABETH. Yes, Sister.

SISTER MARY LUCILLE. Don't use that tone with me, young lady. Sluska, read that note.

WANDA. Do I have to, Sister?

SISTER MARY LUCILLE. Don't defy Sister, read that note.

WANDA. "Sister Lucy plays bongo drums with Monsignor Ricardo in the closet."

SISTER MARY LUCILLE. Now, I would like you two to diagram this sentence for homework, one hundred times. As a matter of fact, the whole class can do it so nobody gets itchy fingers. Write that note on the blackboard, Miss Sluska.

MARIA THERESA. Thanks a lot, you guys.

SISTER MARY LUCILLE. P.S., girls, not funny. (*ELIZABETH sneezes. This is the signal to start humming the theme song from a popular '50's TV sit-com.*) The theme for the dance will be. . . . stop that this instant or there won't be a dance. (*humming stops*) The theme for the dance will be "Spring Flowers." Now, as for the chaperones, we will need four to handle this crowd, plus the faculty. Maria Theresa, how about your father? He is a nice, big, beefy man and your sisters always brought him.

MARIA THERESA. I think he will be working nights then, Sister.

SISTER MARY LUCILLE. I think he can get off for just one night, right, Miss Russo?

MARIA THERESA. Yes, Sister.

SISTER MARY LUCILLE. Miss Sluska, we expect a cold cut donation from your father. A few rules for the dance. No Beatles music. You will not bring any of the filth that is running around, outside the school, via the dance. None of the long hair, the cigarettes, or those Brits from Liverpool who run around saying that they are better than Jesus Christ. Also it is semi-formal. That means, girls, no mini skirts, no long gowns . . .

MARIA THERESA. But I just finished my last payment.

SISTER MARY LUCILLE. Please, girls, no fishnet stockings, no make up, no jewelry and perhaps some wrist-length white gloves. Boys, jackets, white shirts and navy blue ties.

ELIZABETH. I don't believe it. (*She sneezes, class hums.*)

SISTER MARY LUCILLE. Well you better believe it or there won't be a dance. Now, boys and girls, you have heard a rumor about an incident that occurred in my classroom last year. That I took James Fowley's head and smashed it against the blackboard. This is not a rumor, this is a fact. (*humming stops*) That boy provoked me. That boy's parents marched right up to this school and walked through that very classroom door . . . and they thanked me. The same thing will happen to you if there is any sort of misconduct at that dance. No smoking, no drinking, and if there is any slow dancing, I want the couples to dance an arm's length apart. That is enough room for you and the Holy Ghost. Have I made myself clear? HAVE I MADE MYSELF CLEAR?

ALL. Yes, Sister Mary Lucille.

(*All move* D.S.R. *and bunch together at the dance. 1960's dance music is playing.*)

COLLEEN. Look at the boys, they're all squished up there by the band. Nobody is going to dance with us. What a bomb.

WANDA. Well, if nobody asks us to dance, we can dance with each other.

COLLEEN. Like a bunch of lesbos, forget it. If it wasn't for you, Elizabeth, we wouldn't have to wear these stupid uniforms.

ELIZABETH. Hey, Colleen, you were the one who carried it too far. I was just going to put the bongo drums on her desk. You didn't have to play them like an "ass" in the bathroom.

MARIA THERESA. Hey, look, here comes Eddie.

WANDA. First comes love, second comes marriage, then comes Maria and a baby carriage.

ALL. Hi, Eddie. (*They push MARIA THERESA forward but the imaginary EDDIE asks COLLEEN to dance.*)

COLLEEN. Yeah, sure, Eddie, I'd love to. Toodles, faggots. (*COLLEEN dances offstage.*)

WANDA. What a traitor.

MARIA THERESA. I called dibs on Eddie. He was supposed to be mine. I just want to do something to her.

ELIZABETH. Sic your father on her.

MARIA THERESA. Don't mention him.

COLLEEN. (*dancing over to the girls*) Hey, Wanda, I have a message for you. Five o'clock shadow wants to know if you want to dance?

WANDA. Francis?

COLLEEN. That's what I said.

WANDA. Okay, but I'm not dancing anything slow with him, he sweats a lot. (*WANDA Exits.*)

ELIZABETH. Look, Maria . . .

MARIA THERESA. I'm changing my name. Call me Terry.

ELIZABETH. Hey look, Terry, your father is dancing with Lucy.

MARIA THERESA. Arm's length apart, Sister. Perfect couple.

ELIZABETH. Hey, look, they're doing the bunny hop, Maria.

MARIA THERESA. Terry.

ELIZABETH. Hi, Eugene. Let's go do it. He's calling us.

MARIA THERESA. He's calling you.

ELIZABETH. You don't need a partner.

MARIA THERESA. Just go, huh. (*ELIZABETH Exits.*)

COLLEEN. (*from* O.S.) Put your arms around me, Eddie, and you better hop.

MARIA THERESA. (*stands alone listening to music*) Oh hi, Daddy. Get lost, huh? I'm not dancing cause, I don't feel like dancing. I'm in a watching mood. I am not B.S. ing. Don't curse around me, please. I'm having a great time. I just don't want to dance, because my legs are a little tired. I don't want to dance with you. No it's not because you dance weird, no it's not because you're fat. It's because of a guy I know. Which one? That one. Daddy, lower your voice! No, I don't want you to break his legs. Daddy, I got to tell you something. I've always been afraid of you and you've always been afraid of me. How come, huh? All right, I'll dance with you. And Daddy let's bash into Eddie every once in awhile, okay?

(*MARIA THERESA dances awkwardly with her imaginary father,* S.R. *as COLLEEN, WANDA and ELIZABETH do the bunny hop, entering from the left. Finally MARIA THERESA joins them and they "hop" into the classroom scene. WANDA is at the blackboard, erasing. Spring 1970.*)

ELIZABETH. Wanda, Wanda, are you deaf?

MARIA THERESA. Leave her, she's in love.

ELIZABETH. I guess so. Mrs. Francis Crawford, yuch.

MARIA THERESA. My parents went out on a date the other night. To Carlo's.

WANDA. You're kidding.

MARIA THERESA. Nope. And they haven't fought for three days straight. They decided to call the divorce off.

ELIZABETH. (*reading the Encyclopaedia Britannica*) That's great, Maria.

MARIA THERESA. I think she might be having another baby.

WANDA. Your family multiplies like rabbits.

MARIA THERESA. How crude. At least we multiply, only-child-Polack. What's the matter with your mother, huh?

ELIZABETH. Hey, you guys, shut up. After a week of scientific research in Yonker's Public Library, I have found this little tidbit. Ready? (*reads from encyclopaedia*) "The earnest *Jewish* piety of Jesus' home, the character of his parents and especially his mother . . . blah, blah, blah . . . all this helps us to understand the profound religious development of the *man* Christ Jesus. The MAN Christ Jesus.

WANDA. Let me see that. They don't even think Jesus was God.

ELIZABETH. Yeah, I know. And some people don't think there is a God.

MARIA THERESA. They're wrong, right?

WANDA. Are you going to show this to your parents?

ELIZABETH. Nope. I'm copying this and three other

things and I'm going to send them to Sister Mary Lucille.

MARIA THERESA. Are you crazy?

ELIZABETH. I may deliver them personally, depending on her behavior.

WANDA. When?

ELIZABETH. I'll know when the time is right.

WANDA. Yeah, well don't send it till after graduation.

MARIA THERESA. You're taking your life in your hands.

ELIZABETH. I am not.

WANDA. Don't be too sure. (*SISTER MARY LUCILLE Enters.*)

SISTER MARY LUCILLE. Quiet down. I can hear that ruckus all the way across the hall. Sister Mary Agnes won't be in today. . . .

ELIZABETH. Is she all right?

MARIA THERESA. Did she die?

SISTER MARY LUCILLE. She fell on her way from the convent. I will be taking both classes for the day. Oh, does someone want to register a complaint? Just stand right up and say so. Fine, I didn't think so. Elizabeth McHugh pack up your books and get your things together. (*ELIZABETH does so.*) Now I will past out these book reports. Mr. Joseph Ross, "Johnny Tremain" an F. Mr. Ross, it is not sufficient to report on only one page of a book. The page where Johnny Tremain gets his hand encased in silver may hold a fascination with you, but I fail to see this as the outstanding literary event of the 20th Century. No, this won't do. Read the entire book, please. Wanda Sluska, "Atlas Shrugged" by Ian Rand.

WANDA. It's Ayn Rand, Sister.

SISTER LUCILLE. IAN-ayn, Miss Sluska, see me after class. And tell your father, I don't like kidneys.

ELIZABETH. I'm ready.

SISTER MARY LUCILLE. Class, if a girl refuses to learn her lessons, time and time again, God has a way of making his displeasure known. Elizabeth you continue to disobey my will, which is God's will, and therefore he has sent you a personal message of disapproval that I have been entrusted to deliver. Your mother called in to Sister Rose Gertrude and I am sorry to tell you this; but your grandmother passed away this morning.

MARIA THERESA. Elizabeth, I'm sorry.

SISTER MARY LUCILLE. Down in your seat.

ELIZABETH. What time this morning?

SISTER MARY LUCILLE. Keep your mouth quiet.

ELIZABETH. (*softly*) Jesus was a Jew.

SISTER MARY LUCILLE. Excuse me?

ELIZABETH. Jesus was a Jew.

SISTER MARY LUCILLE. Shut it, young lady.

(*SISTER MARY LUCILLE slaps ELIZABETH across her face. ELIZABETH Exits. WANDA stands with the encyclopaedia.*)

WANDA. Jesus was a Jew and I have the facts to back it up.

MARIA THERESA. (*bars the door to the classroom with a pointer*) Jesus really was a Jew, read it, Wanda.

WANDA. "Jesus was the promised Messiah of Jewish expectation, that is, the exalted, semi-divine King of Israel, in the glorious age to come . . ."

SISTER MARY LUCILLE. Who gave you that information?

MARIA THERESA. . . . And Jesus may just be an ordinary, old human. Just a regular guy, sort of smart.

SISTER MARY LUCILLE. Mr. Reynolds, sit down, or I will cut the legs from underneath you. Hand me that book, Sluska.

WANDA. (*tosses the book to MARIA*) Maria. "In the end it was the Jerusalem hierarchy and the officers of the Roman army of occupation who put Jesus to death." Catch, Maria. (*MARIA THERESA catches book.*)

MARIA THERESA. Jesus probably wasn't any good at math, either.

(*MARIA THERESA Exits with the book, SISTER MARY LUCILLE follows her and then WANDA Exits.*)

WANDA. Wait 'till the Pope hears about this.

(*Lights fade as ELIZABETH reenters. Spot light comes up on her.*)

ELIZABETH. (*to God, as if she is in church:*) Hey, come on out, I want to talk to you. It's me, Elizabeth. You can hide behind any statue in this place, but you better listen to me. I don't know if you know this but after my grandmother moved in with us, everything was different. We used to sit in my room, after school. She'd ask me questions about all sorts of things. Then she'd listen to my answers real close because she said I was an important person. Some nights, after we went to bed, I would hear her talking to my grandfather in the dark. If I made any noise she'd stop. Because it was private. One night I saw that she was crying. I made some noise and she stopped. Then she asked me if I remembered my grandfather. I did, she liked that. We fell asleep on her bed like sisters. Sunday mornings were kind of strange. Nobody would give up eating bacon and some smells made her sick. My father would tell her if the grease bothered her so much, to take her eggs and go into the bedroom and wait until breakfast was over. I helped her stuff towels into the cracks under the door; but the smell got in anyway. Then my father would make me come back to the table and eat with the rest of the family. I'd go, but I wouldn't eat that bacon. Sometimes, if she was feeling a little better we'd take short walks. After we had rested, she'd tell me stories about my mother and bring along pictures that I had never seen. I didn't know why my mother was so sad and neither did my grandmother. One day, my father came home from work and told me that my grandmother would have to move back to the Bronx. He said it was just not working out. She needed more care and besides she was making the family crazy. I told him that she wasn't making me crazy. I told him she let me be near her. He didn't understand that. And now I see that you didn't either. You took her and I don't think that's fair. You're supposed to do the right thing, all the time. I don't believe that anymore. You just like to punish people, you like to interrupt their lives. You didn't let me finish. She doesn't know what I think, and I was almost ready to tell her. Why don't you take my mother next time? Oh, you like to take little kids, don't you? Grab one of my brothers next, they're all baptized. Why don't you take my whole stinking family, in one shot, then you won't waste any time. That would be some joke. But I want to tell you something. It's a personal message, I'm delivering it, myself. Don't you ever lay your hands on me, cause if I ever see you, you can strike me dead . . . try . . . I will spit all over your face, whatever it looks like. Because you and everyone else in this world are one big pack of liars. And I really think I hate you. Something else: You don't exist.

(*ELIZABETH turns from audience. Spot out and ELIZ-ABETH Exits. Classroom lights up on SISTER*

MARY AGNES's class. COLLEEN and MARIA THERESA Enter dragging field hockey sticks, followed by ELIZABETH.)

COLLEEN. We got burnt.

MARIA THERESA. How embarrassing. We'll never beat Lucille's homeroom like this. Elizabeth, you let everything fly right by.

COLLEEN. Maria, you didn't do much better. Elizabeth, don't worry.

MARIA THERESA. I'm nervous about the co-ops results. You don't care about them, so what's your excuse, huh?

ELIZABETH. Maria, don't bug me.

COLLEEN. Elizabeth, I beg you, don't give up, don't go to public school. Don't let Lucy ruin your life.

ELIZABETH. It's not her, it's him. You know if you are a Catholic and you have something you like, he . . .

MARIA THERESA. He who?

ELIZABETH. God.

MARIA THERESA. Oh.

ELIZABETH. He finds out about it and then he takes it away. Just to punish you. So I don't care about anything, anymore.

COLLEEN. Oh, that's not true. God is going to let you into Saint Mary's.

ELIZABETH. No, he's not.

MARIA THERESA. I agree with Elizabeth.

ELIZABETH. You do?

MARIA THERESA. Yup. How come I'm always failing math, huh? Punishment.

COLLEEN. Punishment for what?

MARIA THERESA. I don't know. (*SISTER MARY AGNES Enters.*)

SISTER MARY AGNES. Girls, your minds were not on the game. Eight to . . . humm . . . to what?

MARIA THERESA. Eight to one. Ask her.

COLLEEN. Sister, the reason we couldn't concentrate is because, well, the co-op admission slips are in the mail today. And we were wondering if we could get out a little early to call our mothers.

SISTER MARY AGNES. (*looks around in her shopping bag*) Well, I don't know, you girls are so noisy by that phone.

COLLEEN. Sister, you have to. I'm going to kill myself if I have to wait till three o'clock.

MARIA THERESA. I'll take names.

COLLEEN. Have a heart.

SISTER MARY AGNES. What was I looking for?

MARIA THERESA. A phone.

SISTER MARY AGNES. A bone. Oh no, a foot, yes. Here is a rabbit's foot for each of you to hold on to, while you are on the phone. Mary Steven, (*to MARIA THERESA:*) you get two, you're going to need them.

MARIA THERESA. Thanks, Sister. That's sweet.

COLLEEN. You're a sly devil, Sister.

SISTER MARY AGNES. Don't thank me, thank Rufus. It was all his idea.

MARIA THERESA. Thanks, Rufus.

COLLEEN. Thanks, Rufus, can we go, Sister?

SISTER MARY AGNES. Yes, but be quiet by that phone.

(*MARIA THERESA, COLLEEN Exit, ELIZABETH hesitates.*)

COLLEEN. Elizabeth, come on.

SISTER MARY AGNES. Get going, dear, don't forget your rabbit's foot, Loretta.

ELIZABETH. I don't care about dumb old Saint Mary's. And I don't believe in magic.

SISTER MARY AGNES. What do you believe in, dear?

ELIZABETH. Facts. I think it's only fair to tell you that I am not a Catholic anymore, Sister. God hates me and I hate God. Sister Agnes, you're really nice for a nun and all, but you're all wrong about God.

SISTER MARY AGNES. What do you mean?

ELIZABETH. God is just a killer. He killed my grandmother and he killed Rufus. You probably forgave him, but I never will. Never.

SISTER MARY AGNES. That's up to you. Stay angry, as long as you like. But I've got some bad news: God will never give up on you. And I don't think you'll be able to keep that heart of yours closed forever.

ELIZABETH. Don't bet on it, Sister. (*ELIZABETH begins to Exit.*)

SISTER MARY AGNES. Elizabeth, you forgot something.

ELIZABETH. What?

SISTER MARY AGNES. Your rabbit's foot, dear. (*ELIZABETH takes it and Exits.*)

COLLEEN. (*lights up on phone area*) Stop pushing, will you? Don't you have any class?

MARIA THERESA. Good luck, Eddie. (*WANDA Enters area.*)

WANDA. Who's got change of a quarter?

COLLEEN. Oh, God. Glad you could make it, Elizabeth.

ELIZABETH. I didn't have a choice. I didn't feel like listening to her singing and talking to Rufus.

COLLEEN. Who's first? Not me, that's for sure. Maria, you go ahead, you first. Come on dial, I'm dying.

MARIA THERESA. Hello, Mom, Dad? Daddy, how

come you're home from work? Nothing's wrong? I just wanted to call and see if the mail was there yet, Daddy. Daddy, let Mom get it please. They're fighting to see who gets to open it. Ma, hi, yeah, what does it say? I got in. I'm real glad. No, tell him I'll talk to him later . . . Ma, there are other people waiting. Hi, Dad, yeah, I got in. Gotta go. I did it. I made it. Go ahead, Wanda.

WANDA. Tak man. Jestem bardzo podniecona. Czy otrzymalam stypendium? Skad?

ELIZABETH. She doesn't show any expression.

WANDA. Ze Swietej marit Swieteco Ignaca. Wspaniale. Do Zubaczenia.

COLLEEN. She probably got a scholarship.

WANDA. Kocham cie. . . . Five hundred bucks.

COLLEEN. Big deal. Hi, Mom. It's me. Me, Colleen. Brian, get off the extension. Yuch, he coughed right in my ear. What a freak. Did you get the mail yet? No, Mom, go get it. She didn't get the mail yet, can you believe her? Not Daddy's mail, my mail. Can't you be serious, stop kidding around. Open it up, what does it say? Okay, 'bye. All four schools!

MARIA THERESA. Which one are you going to?

COLLEEN. Saint Mary's, of course. Elizabeth, go ahead.

MARIA THERESA. Our Father, Who art in Heaven. . . .

ELIZABETH. Cut it out, Maria, it's already decided. Mom, hi. Did you get the mail yet? Open it. I didn't? 'Bye, Mommy.

WANDA. Oh, Elizabeth.

COLLEEN. Shit. (*covers her mouth quickly*)

ELIZABETH. (*steps away from girls, looking very sad*) then . . . I'm kidding. I did.

ALL. Saint Mary's, here we come.

*(COLLEEN, MARIA THERESA, WANDA return to
their desks, pack up their books, listening while
ELIZABETH speaks in monologue spot.)*

ELIZABETH. So that's it, I guess. Except that a couple
of weeks ago, I was at a party. For some reason I began
telling all these wild Catholic school stories. I hadn't
thought about that part of my life, for a long time, but all
the memories came back. We laughed for hours. Then as
I was leaving, someone I didn't know very well, a public
school refugee, asked me what I thought about God,
now. I said I didn't think anything about Him except that
maybe He wasn't a guy and left. When I got home, I
couldn't get to sleep. The tail end of "Miracle on 34th
Street" was on. The little girl was driving in a car and she
had her eyes shut tight. She was saying over and over in
the sweetest MGM voice, "I believe, I believe," over and
over. I turned it off. I pulled my blanket up and I shut my
eyes tight. I remembered how I used to believe in miracles, falling asleep with some question in my mind. And
that night, it seemed the whole process was beginning
again. Because I found myself asking, into the dark dis-
tance, a vaguely familiar question, "Are you there, Are
you there?"

(Lights come down slowly on ELIZABETH.)

THE END

COSTUME PLOT

ACT I

White cotton slips (4)
White Peter Pan Collar Long Sleeved Uniform Blouses
  (4)
Navy Blue Ties (4)
Navy Blue Knee Socks (4 pairs)
Brown Oxford Shoes (4 pairs)
Green/Blue Plaid Uniform Jumper with Detachable
  Upper Bib (4)

ACT II

Detach Upper Bib so Pleated Skirt Remains (4)

PROPERTY LIST

ACT I

FIRST GRADE:
Apple
Holy Medal
Statue of Jesus Christ
Holy Water

SECOND GRADE:
Candy
Construction Paper
Halloween Decorations
Mission Box
Crayola Crayons
Cray-pas
Ruler
John F. Kennedy's Portrait

FOURTH GRADE:
Classroom Monitor's Book (on chain)
Go-Go Boots
Baton
Streamers
Bubbles
Feather Boa (4)
Trophy
Money
Math Text Books (4)
Math Homework
Ball Point Pen
Paper Airplane

ACT II

SIXTH GRADE:
Tampon
Glass of Water
True Confessions
Sanitary Napkin Kits (4)

EIGHTH GRADE:
Transistor Radio (with earphone)
Sunglasses
Shopping Bag
Holy Water
Text Books
Lesson Plan Book
Eyeglasses (on chain)

EIGHTH GRADE (SPRING):
Encyclopaedia Britannica
Field Hockey Sticks (4)
Rabbit's Foot (4)

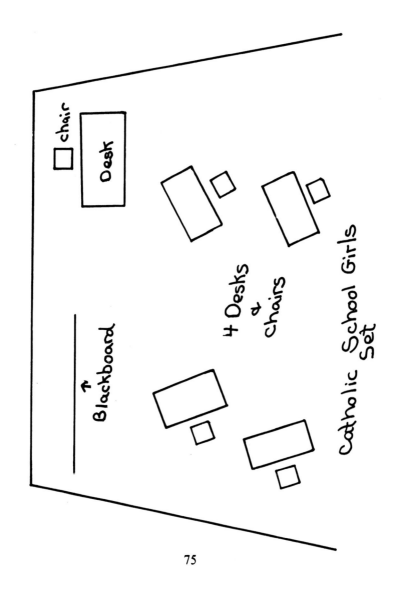

chair

Desk

Blackboard →

4 Desks
&
Chairs

Catholic School Girls
Set

Also By

Casey Kurtti

THREE WAYS HOME

OTHER TITLES AVAILABLE FROM SAMUEL FRENCH

BLUE YONDER
Kate Aspengren

Dramatic Comedy / Monolgues and scenes
12f (can be performed with as few as 4 with doubling) / Unit Set

A familiar adage states, "Men may work from sun to sun, but women's work is never done." In Blue Yonder, the audience meets twelve mesmerizing and eccentric women including a flight instructor, a firefighter, a stuntwoman, a woman who donates body parts, an employment counselor, a professional softball player, a surgical nurse professional baseball player, and a daredevil who plays with dynamite among others. Through the monologues, each woman examines her life's work and explores the career that she has found. Or that has found her.

CPSIA information can be obtained at www.ICGtesting.com
Printed in the USA
BVOW05s1658240214

345850BV00017B/831/P